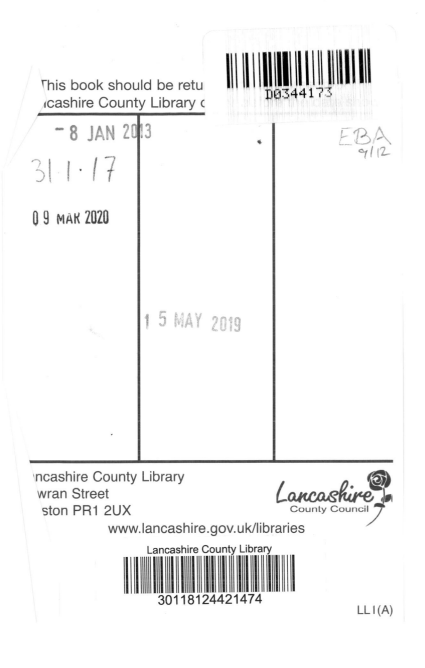

# Bad Rat!

Written by Karen Wallace
Illustrated by Rachael O'Neill

WISE WALRUS

# What is synthetic phonics?

**Synthetic phonics** teaches children to recognise the sounds of letters and to blend 'synthesise' them together to make whole words.

Understanding sound/letter relationships gives children the confidence and ability to read unfamiliar words, without having to rely on memory or guesswork; this helps them progress towards independent reading.

**Did you know?** Spoken English uses more than 40 speech sounds. Each sound is called a *phoneme*. Some phonemes relate to a single letter (d-o-g) and others to combinations of letters (sh-ar-p). When a phoneme is written down it is called a *grapheme*. Teaching these sounds, matching them to their written form and sounding out words for reading is the basis of synthetic phonics.

# Consultant

*I love reading phonics* has been created in consultation
with language expert Dr Marlynne Grant (Chartered
and Registered Educational Psychologist). For more than
25 years, Marlynne has worked as a regional educational
psychologist, specialising in literacy development for
children of all abilities.

# Reading tips

*Bad Rat!* focuses on the sounds:
**s, a, t, p, i, n, c, e, h, r, m, d, g, o, u, l, f** and **b**.

## Tricky words in *Bad Rat!*

Any words in bold do not sound exactly as they look
(don't fit the usual sound–letter rules) or are new and
have not yet been introduced.

| Tricky words in this book: | | | |
|---|---|---|---|
| **my** | **s<u>ai</u>d** | **to** | <u>**the**</u> |
| <u>**I**</u> | **s<u>ee</u>** | **y<u>ou</u>** | **m<u>e</u>** |

## Extra ways to have fun with *Bad Rat!*

• After the reader has read the story, ask them questions
about what they have just read:

*Where did Rat hide?*
*Why was Rat's behaviour bad?*

• Make flashcards of the focus sounds (s, a, t, p, i, n, c,
e, h, r, m, d, g, o, u, l, f and b). Ask the reader to say the
sounds. This will help reinforce letter/sound matches.

Reading is fun!
I love to read with my mum,
snuggled up in bed. She always
says *"Well done!"*
when I read.

# A pronunciation guide

 This grid contains the sounds used in the story and a guide on how to say them.

| | | |
|---|---|---|
| s<br>as in sat | a<br>as in ant | t<br>as in tin |
| p<br>as in pig | i<br>as in ink | n<br>as in net |
| c<br>as in cat | e<br>as in egg | h<br>as in hen |
| r<br>as in rat | m<br>as in mug | d<br>as in dog |
| g<br>as in get | o<br>as in ox | u<br>as in up |
| l<br>as in log | f<br>as in fan | b<br>as in bag |

Be careful not to add an 'uh' sound to 's', 't', 'p', 'c', 'h', 'r', 'm', 'd', 'g', 'l', 'f' and 'b'. For example, say 'fff' not 'fuh' and 'sss' not 'suh'.

Rat hid a bun in his bed.

'**My** bun!' **said** Pig **to** Fat Cat.

'**The** bad rat has **my** bun!'

'Let **me** get Rat!' **said** Fat Cat.

Fat Cat ran **to the** red hut.

Rat hid in a pot!

Rat hid in a hat!

Rat hid in a mug!

Fat Cat sat on **the** rug.

'I can **see you**, Rat,' **said** Fat Cat.
Tug! Tug!

'Get **me the** bun, Rat. Pig is mad,'
**said** Fat Cat.

'**The** bun is in **the** bed,' **said** Rat.

Pig has his bun.

Bad Rat!

## Other **Level 1** titles to enjoy:

978-1-84898-391-5

978-1-84898-390-8

978-1-84898-396-0

**Other titles in the series**

### Level **2**

978-1-84898-386-1

978-1-84898-387-8

978-1-84898-388-5

978-1-84898-389-2

### Level **3**

978-1-84898-397-7

978-1-84898-398-4

978-1-84898-399-1

978-1-84898-400-4

Copyright © Wise Walrus Ltd 2011
First published in Great Britain in 2011 by Wise Walrus
The Pantiles Chambers, 85 High Street, Tunbridge Wells, Kent TN1 1XP
ISBN: 978-1-84898-277-2
Printed in China 10 9 8 7 6 5 4 3 2 1